OLIVIA™
and the Babies

adapted by Jodie Shepherd
based on the screenplay "Mother of the Year"
written by Eryk Casemiro and Kate Boutilier
illustrated by Jared Osterhold

SIMON AND SCHUSTER

Based on the TV series OLIVIA™

First published in Great Britain in 2010 by Simon and Schuster UK Ltd
1st Floor, 222 Gray's Inn Road, London, WC1X 8HB
A CBS Company

Published in the United States by Little Simon, an imprint of Simon & Schuster Children's Publishing Division

ISBN: 978-1-84738-791-2

Printed in Great Britain

10 9 8 7 6 5 4 3 2 1

www.simonandschuster.co.uk

Olivia, Ian, Baby William, and their mother had all gone to the market to shop for food.

A woman approached the shopping trolley. "Coochie coochie coo," she said, tickling Baby William under his chin. "What an adorable little baby!"

"Thank you," said Mummy. "Yes, he is!"

"Aren't you handsome?" another shopper said to the baby. "You should be in the movies, yes you should!"

"He is a handsome one," replied Mummy. "I think I'll keep him."

"Pinto beans, garbanzo beans, beans-that-kids-should-never-have-to-eat beans," Olivia mumbled. "Mum, can we buy corn instead? Mum?"

Meanwhile, Ian was trying to decide which cereal to buy. "This one is crunchy, but there's no toy," he said to himself. "This one comes with free stick-on tattoos, but it has those gross little marshmallow things. And this one – yuck! – it gets soggy. So which should I choose? OLIVIA!"

"Look at those dimples, that smile, and oh, what a nose!" said a grocery store worker. "You must be a happy mother."
"I am," Mummy answered. "Thank you."

"Ahem. M-u-m," Olivia repeated, looking at the baby. "Can we buy corn instead of beans?"
"Hmm," Olivia thought. "Baby William really *is* cute."

"Olivia, which cereal?" Ian repeated.
"I can't think about cereal right now, Ian," Olivia told her brother. "I've decided I'm going to be a mummy, and I've got a lot to do."

Back home, Olivia's new baby kept her busy. "Any letters for me, Mr Mailman," she asked, "or for my baby, Little Olivia?"

"Oh my goodness," said the mailman. "He's a cute one, he is."

"Yes, he is cute," Olivia agreed. "I think I'll keep him."

"My, my, isn't he a vision of loveliness?" Mrs Hogenmuller said admiringly as she passed by.

"Yes, he is," Olivia agreed again. She kissed Little Olivia on the nose. "Who's Mummy's pretty baby?" she cooed.

"One baby is so much fun," Olivia thought.

"I wonder what it would be like to have two babies . . ."

"What would Mummy's favourite babies like to do today?" asked Olivia. "Oh, hi, Francine. I was so busy with Little Olivia and Little Olivia Two that I didn't notice you there. They're such a handful."

"Oh, wow! They're so cute," gushed Francine. "I think I'd like to be a mummy too."

"Meet Franny, my baby," said Francine. "She's a little fussy today."
"Maybe she needs a nap," Olivia suggested. "Maybe she's tired."

"It's not her naptime," Francine answered. "Babies just act fussy sometimes."

"Hey, Olivia!" shouted Francine. "Make your babies behave! Your babies are causing trouble."

"Little Olivia Two, get back in your buggy!" Olivia said firmly. She turned to Francine. "He's not misbehaving; he is just getting some exercise."

"HELP!" Francine shouted. "Franny, come to Mummy!"
Olivia stayed calm. "I'm sorry to say this, Francine, but I think it would be best if Franny didn't play with my babies today."
"Bye, Olivia!" said Francine.

Back home, Olivia had just put her babies down for a nap when Mum asked for her help.

Olivia agreed to watch William while her mother was on the phone . . . as long as she could call him Little Olivia Three. William didn't seem to mind.

Just when everything was peaceful, Ian came into the room and woke up
all three babies.
"Now how am I going to take care of all my babies at the same time?"
Olivia thought. Then she had an idea . . .

Roller skates!

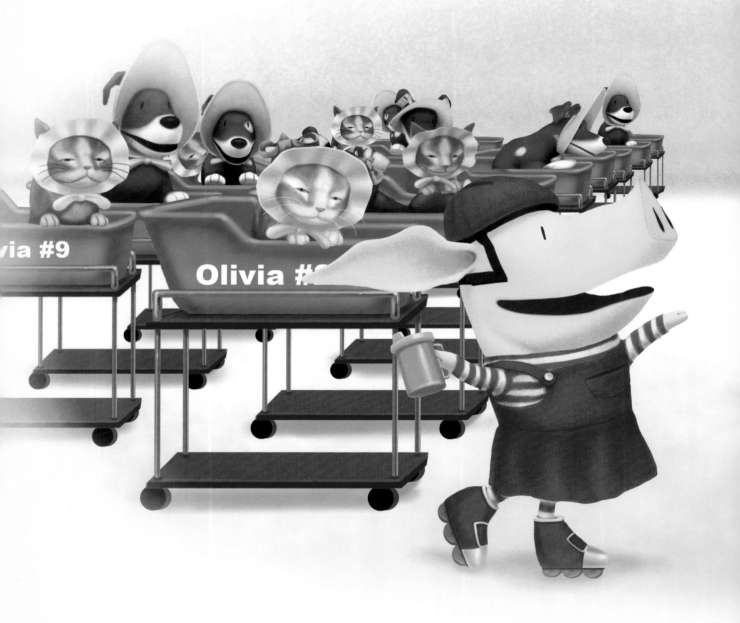

Little Olivia Three was in tears.

"Wheee! Wheee!" called Olivia. "Look at me, Little Olivia Three!"

Little Olivia Three stopped crying and started to giggle! Mummies can be so silly!

That night Olivia was really tired!
"I'm really proud of you, Olivia,"
said her mother.
"Thank you, Mum," Olivia replied.
"But being a mummy is a lot of
work. I think I'll wait until I'm
old – like you."
Olivia's mother smiled.
"And I'm sure when you
have babies of your own
you will be mother
of the year! Good
night, Olivia."